Call Him Daddy

A DARK AGE GAP BILLIONAIRE ROMANCE

KATIE A PEREZ

 Created with Vellum

If you wanted a book with plot- stop here.

If you came for smutty, age gap novella-
Daddy Theo is ready for you,
So be a good girl and turn the page.

This book has several open-door and explicit sexual scenes. It is not intended for anyone under the age of 18.
There are also mentions of some heavy topics including but not limited to :
Cheating (not between MMC & FMC)
Drugging (not between MMC & FMC)
Abuse (Verbal from parent)
Degradation
If these are things that will adversely affect your mental health, please close the book now.

https://open.spotify.com/embed/playlist/
70tThGnC10KntNxXz9NjgD?utm_source=generator

I Wanna Be Yours- Arctic Monkeys
Habits(Stay High)-Tove Lo
THE DEATH OF PIECE OF MIND- Bad Omens
Daddy Issues- The Neighborhood
i like the way you kiss me-Artemas
older- Isabel LaRosa
Too Sweet- Hozier
favorite- Isabel LaRosa
i'm yours- Isabel LaRosa
eyes don't lie-Isabel LaRosa
Softcore-The Neighborhood
Sweater Weather- The Neighborhood
LET THE WORLD BURN- Chris Gray
Make You Mine- Madison Beer
love me-Ex Habit
Good Luck, Babe!- Chappell Roan
THE RIDE- Omido, Kae
Good Girls Go Bad- Cobra Strarship, Leighton
Meester

Prologue

"THREE, TWO, ONE!" the crowd roars as confetti cannons shower us in pink paper.

The largest smile I've ever had crosses my face as I reach out for Alana. Her blonde curls bounce over her shoulder. I pull her close to me as she stands with her hands over her mouth and tears start to stream down her cheeks.

My arms wrap around her as she rests her face on my chest.

"We're having a mini you," I whisper into her hair, and her body shudders against me.

Moments later, all of our family rushes us, drowning us with excitement. Alana gets pulled away by her sister. I step back out of the mob of people offering their congratulations to where some of my best friends are standing off to the side.

Donavon hands me a beer as he claps my shoulder. "Congrats, Theo. Girl dad, that's,"—he takes a drink from his open bottle—"something."

I snort. "You don't need to pretend you're happy for me. Just because I'm settling down and having kids doesn't mean you have to," I laugh as I take a drink of my own.

"You're twenty-one; you haven't even lived yet ." He gives me a knowing look.

Donavan and I have been friends since we were in diapers. We were inseparable until Luke moved next door when we were seven. That was when it became the three of us. Now it's three peas in a pod.

"Are you even sure the thing is yours?" he asks next, a question that makes my blood boil.

My hand grips my beer tighter as I struggle to swallow the liquid in my mouth. "What the fuck, man? I understand you don't like her, but she is my future wife and the mother of my unborn daughter. Have some fucking respect," I seethe.

He just shakes his head. "Fuck this, man. You were so close to getting out of here, but you let her get in the way of you doing something with your life. When you told her about the job opportunities, she said she wasn't ready to leave her hometown. You were going to go without her, and we supported that.

"You worked so hard to make those connections, then suddenly she's pregnant? The timing is a bit convenient, don't you think? And isn't it weird Luke hasn't even tried to congratulate you today? For someone who is supposed to be your best friend, he doesn't even offer a half-hearted congrats?"

My eyes narrow into slits as I address him. "What the fuck are you implying, Don?"

His lips thin. "Everyone knows he's been in love with Alana since middle school."

"And? He never had an issue with me being with her before," I snap.

He scoffs outright, "Yeah, because he has been fucking her the whole time."

My body tenses as I fight to keep myself from causing a

scene. "Get out," I snarl. "Get the fuck out." Everyone is now looking over at us, noticing the commotion.

Don raises his hands as he starts backing away. "Just figured you should know before you ruin your future."

I watch as he walks out the front gate and listen for the rev of his motorcycle before looking back to the party. Luckily, it doesn't seem like anyone heard his comments.

A gentle hand is placed on my arm, making me look to the side.

"Are you okay?" Alana asks quietly, her green eyes filled with worry.

"I'll be fine." I shake my arm out of her grip. I don't believe what he said. There is no way Alana would do something like that, but feeling her touch is making my stomach flip. I need to just take a minute to calm down and rejoin the celebration. "I'll be back."

Taking a deep breath and nodding to some relatives and friends nearby, I walk into the house before heading straight to the bathroom. I stand with my hands against the cold granite counter with my head hung low.

In the four years Alana and I have been together, there has never been a second I didn't trust her. In the fourteen years I have been friends with Luke, we have never fought over a girl.

None of this makes sense, but I can't shake the uneasy feeling in my gut. The overpowering sense that something is *wrong*. Bile rises in my throat.

I was aware of the baby-trapping rumor but, whether it was true or not, it didn't change how I felt about her and our daughter.

Never once did it occur to me that this baby could be anyone else's. *Never.*

I take a deep breath before pushing off the counter. I'm going to put on a smile, finish the party, and have a discussion

3

with Alana tonight. There's been enough of a scene today, and I don't need to make things worse.

I open the bathroom door, but before I can even take a full step out into the hallway, a hushed conversation catches my attention.

"I told you no. There will be no test. Theo is the father." *Alana.* I freeze.

"You don't just get to decide that. I can provide you with a beautiful life, too, ya know. You can't just keep my daughter away from me." *Luke*... fuck.

"She is not your daughter, Luke. She's Theo's," Alana hisses back.

My heart is hammering as he replies, "That's not how paternity works, Lana, and you know it."

"Luke," she says, her voice softer now.

"If your life with him was so perfect, why did you keep running back to me? You're going to choose him over me because of money?" He pauses.

I lean out of the doorway a little further to see them. My hand grips the door frame, my fingers digging into the drywall as I see Alana pressed up against the wall by Luke. The moment his lips make contact with her neck, I can no longer contain my rage.

"Get the fuck off my fiancée!" I shout down the hall.

Alana gasps as Luke pulls away. There is no remorse on his face as he turns to face me.

Luke just scoffs. "So me kissing her is where you draw the line? Where has this anger been for the last four years? Did you not know that the entire time you were dating her, I was fucking her? You were so busy working that you never figured out she was coming to me every time you worked late?"

I look at Alana to see the shame written across her face. You cannot be fucking serious.

4

"Is he telling the truth?" I try to calm my tone, but it still comes out harsh.

Alana looks past me, and I peer over my shoulder to see our friends and family crowded inside, hearing the entire conversation.

Her eyes meet mine as a lone tear falls down her cheek. My confirmation.

"You need to get the fucking test," I seethe through my teeth.

"I will," she stammers, "and it will show you are her father, and we will be such a beautiful family."

Fuck that. I almost laugh in her face. "No."

Her face drops. "What?" Alana whispers.

"Whether I am her father or not, this is over. If the test comes back and she is mine, I will fight you with everything I have for custody. But if she's not, I will never see you again."

"Theo!" she cries out as I shove past her, walking out the front door as everyone present for the gender reveal party witnesses my shame.

And my breaking heart.

Two Weeks Later

Theo Reeves is excluded as the biological father of Baby Girl Doe.

CHAPTER

One

THEO

How coming home to handle my mother's estate turned into my fist being wrapped in the blonde hair of a woman half my age in a dingy bar bathroom, I'm not sure, but I'm not one to turn down a good time.

I pull her head back, lifting her chest off the sink. Her top is still pulled down, letting me watch her breasts bounce with every thrust in the mirror.

"That pretty pussy is taking my cock so well," I breathe against her neck. Her entire body stiffens, arching back against me. "You like being told how well you're doing, don't you?" I laugh.

Her eyes close as she gently nods. The little noises she's making are just begging me for more. She's trying so hard to stay quiet, but it's only encouraging me to get her to moan my name.

She may not want the entire bar to know what is going on, but I do.

I have been the talk of this town for so long that I might as well give them something new to talk about. A show, if you will. And a fucking good one.

"Why are you hiding such beautiful noises, Baby? I want to hear how I'm affecting you," I tease.

She tries to shake her head 'No', but I tighten my grip on her hair, keeping her eyes on my reflection. I slowly pull my cock out of her, just leaving the tip teasing her entrance.

Her body trembles, her lips breathing a curse.

"If you want to cum, you have to earn it." I smile at her reflection as I can see the battle in her eyes. The desperation of finishing warring with the possibility of everyone at the bar knowing she is bent over the bathroom sink, being used like a whore.

I can see the moment she makes up her mind, and my cock throbs.

"Please," she whispers—music to my ears.

"Please what?" I slowly press back inside her, enjoying every second of her strangling my cock.

"Make me cum," she gasps.

"A little louder, Baby, I can't hear you," I tease, my voice low against her neck.

"Please make me cum." She finally pleads.

"Good girl." I slam into her all the way, bottoming out and pulling her head to the side. Her moans fill the room. "That's what I like to fucking hear."

I pump into her a few more times as her body shakes. I slowly pull myself out of her, letting the waves of her orgasm subside. Her head drops as I release my grip on her hair. She begins to relax as she holds herself up against the sink and lifts her head, meeting my gaze in our reflection. She stares as I wrap my fist around my dick, pumping slowly, gently biting her bottom lip.

"You didn't think we were done yet, did you?" Her eyes flick up to mine as a smile begins to form on her lips. "On your knees, Baby."

She stands and faces me, slowly pulling her pants up, never once breaking eye contact with me. When she goes to fix her shirt, I shake my head. She immediately stops.

"Such a good listener." She slowly descends my body until she is kneeling before me. I pump my dick one more time, sliding my hand through her slickness still on me. "Clean yourself off of me." Her hand replaces mine, slowly gripping my shaft. Her eyes close as she tilts her head to the side, bringing her tongue to the base of my cock and sliding it to the tip, licking up her arousal. Her lips press against my tip before enveloping it. I tense as her tongue wraps around me, sucking every last drop of her cum off. I slide my dick out of her mouth, leaving it pressed up against her lips. Placing my thumb on her chin, I tilt her head up to look at me.

"Do you like the way you taste?" She nods. "Good girl. Open up." Her jaw drops open, and I thrust my cock back in, hitting her throat.

Her body tenses, but she doesn't fight me. I thrust in again harder, and this time she gags. I repeat the motion a few more times, watching her breasts bounce with each thrust. Pumping in and out a few more times, tears begin to fall from her eyes.

"Make me cum, Baby, show me what that pretty mouth can do."

CHAPTER
Two

ARIA

I watch as the bathroom door closes behind Theo and lock the deadbolt before turning around and facing the mirror. I barely recognize my own reflection. Not that I look different from before getting mind-blowingly fucked by a stranger, but from the girl I was growing up. It's hard to imagine that the sweet girl with bows in her hair has turned into this absolute mess.

I fix my shirt before filling my mouth with water from the sink, I rinse away any trace of the extremely attractive tattooed man from my mouth, before wiping away the smeared lipstick. There is not a huge crowd for me to slip into tonight, so I should take advantage of this post fuck adrenaline before it disappears. Is it really a walk of shame if my head is held high? It's not like this is the worst gossip about me that this town has spread. Life has become more fun since I decided that if the town was going to talk, I would give them something to talk about.

A final deep breath has me pushing off the counter and

turning back toward the door. I unlock it and pull it open, walking out into the hallway and heading toward the bar to close my tab.

The blonde that has been serving me all night, and I'm sure I have seen on campus a few times, comes over, "The gentleman who, uh, *disappeared* with you, paid your tab." She laughs to herself. Her cheeks flush slightly, not in judgment, but amusement.

"Thanks. Is he a regular?" I ask. I have been here almost every weekend since coming home, but only when the dance floor is open. Tonight, just the bar is open, bringing in a very different crowd.

"Nope, never seen him before, but he paid with cash. Hundred-dollar bills."

"Multiple? What the fuck did he order? "

"Jameson and Dr. Pepper. His bill was under $50 even after covering your drinks. He handed me 2 bills and said to keep the change. Thought I was getting a shit tip until I saw the extra zero." She finishes wiping the counter down by me. "Speaking of tips," she laughs, "was he as generous a tipper with you?"

I can't help but smile as my cheeks flush, "Very." We both laugh before an older man catcalls her from the other side of the bar.

She stands a little taller when a female voice is heard making a scene out the front doors.

"Catcall or Karen, either seems like a win/win for me." She rolls her eyes before faking a smile. "Be careful heading out, our bouncers are off tonight since we don't get big crowds on Thursdays."

"Thanks. You need me to stay until that guy leaves?" I ask, not wanting to leave her in a bad situation.

"Nah, he's harmless, annoying, but harmless. But thanks, I appreciate it."

"Hey, we have to look out for each other," I smile before she walks away. I pat my pockets, finding my cards and keys before heading out. If someone is causing a scene out front, I don't want to linger longer than necessary. Heading toward the front door, the woman's voice gets louder, and I start to recognize it.

"Alana." Theo's voice is calm but stern, "This is not the time nor the place."

"Why won't you tell me? If you're as successful as you said you were going to be, why not tell me?" My mother's voice slurs, and now it's my eyes rolling to the back of my head. I take a deep breath before continuing out the door.

"Mom!" I scold. Both sets of eyes shoot at me.

"Aria. There you are!" She's still pissed. I was hoping she would be more level-headed after some time apart, but it looks like we both thought liquor was the answer. Too bad a single glass of rosé has her drunk.

"You act like I was lost." I continue walking toward her, and Theo's stare has not moved. "Please tell me you didn't drive."

"Contrary to what you may think, I am not that stupid." She stumbles as she crosses her arms over her chest.

Theo glances back and forth between the two of us before looking back at me, "How old are you?"

Slightly stunned, I look at him a moment before responding, "Twenty-two."

I can see gears turning behind his eyes. He lifts his head, looking up to the sky before dragging his palms across his face. He mutters, "Fuck." But not in the sexy way he had while my lips were wrapped around his cock.

"Does it matter?" I ask. I am younger than him, but still an adult, able to consent to everything we just did.

"No." His tone is short. "But lose my number."

"Wait, what? Why?" My mom is swaying between the two of us, nearly falling every time she turns her head.

"This is something you need to talk to your mother about when she is," he looks at her with pure hatred before finishing his sentence, "sober."

Before I have a chance to ask him anything else, he's gone. Somehow, my mother has ruined yet another, good thing in my life. You would think after completely fucking up my childhood, the least she could do is leave my social life, as an adult, alone.

"Get in the car. I don't want to hear a single word out of your mouth tonight, but tomorrow you will explain to me what the fuck just happened."

She feigns offense, "Aria Mason! You do not speak to your mother in that tone!"

"You may be my mother, but I owe you no respect." I slam the door as she continues to stare daggers at me. I should have never come back home after college. I should have stayed in my cute little studio apartment until I got a job offer anywhere but here.

CHAPTER
Three

THEO

Aria. *Fucking*. Mason.

Of course, who else would it be? My jaw tightens as the whiskey continues to circle the inside of my glass. The second she called Alana 'mom', I could see the resemblance. I always knew I had a type, but damn. What's worse is that, now that she is completely off-limits, I can't stop thinking about her. The way the neon reflected in her green eyes, or how her perfect pouty lips looked wrapped around my cock. *Fuck*, I cannot be thinking of her like that. If I hadn't walked out of the bathroom when I did, I would have raised her and been her father. But I'm not. The first time I saw her was last night when she walked up to the bar. I never saw her as a child. I never held her as an infant. Who her mother is should not affect my attraction to her. If I back away, isn't that what I'm doing? Letting her relationship with my ex-fiance affect the feelings I have toward her? What *are* the feelings I have toward her? We had thirty minutes of conversation and a good fuck. We exchanged numbers in case we wanted to go another round, but it's not like we would ever have a real relationship. She's only fucking twenty-two.

My fists tighten around the glass until I feel it start to give. I put it down on the table beside my chair, and switch it out with my phone. I have been ignoring it for long enough. After last night, I needed time to clear my head before doing any work. I cannot be distracted and make a mistake. Even a minor fuck up can cost me everything.

The screen lights up, and I start scrolling through all the missed notifications. Several company emails that I approved last week, a couple of report updates that Eddy should be handling, a text from an unknown number, and a bunch of spam. The only thing pulling my attention is the text. I don't get random texts from unknown numbers, which has me thinking it has to be Aria. Why would I think she would follow my explicit instruction to lose my number and not contact me? She is too feisty to give up that easily. Her spunk was one of the things that drew me to her, along with how she criticized everything about this place. I hoped coming back to town after this long, so many things would have changed, especially with how much infrastructure has been built in the last twenty years. But somehow, this small town has held onto absolutely every trait that made it the worst place to be.

I open my messages and click on the unknown number.

> What the fuck was that, Theo?

> Really? Not going to answer?

> What happened in the 5 minutes it took me to close out my tab that had you running scared?

It's cute that she thinks I was scared. No, sweet girl, I was pissed. It's hard not to become incredibly angry at the sight of the ex who attempted to baby-trap you with another man's child. Anger doesn't even seem like a strong enough word. I had hoped that during this little trip home, I wouldn't even have to hear her name, let alone see her.

> Fine ghost me, Asshole

> I'm still reeling from last night. Round 2? Or would it be considered 3?

> Well if you're not going to answer I'll find someone else to fuck me tonight

I stare at the last message. It was sent thirty minutes ago. I could respond and tell her no one else is allowed to touch her. But that implies I'll fuck her again. As much as I want to, I shouldn't. Her body may have been designed just for me, with the way she took my cock so perfectly, but I cannot get wrapped up in Alana's daughter. I do not want another run-in with her or Luke.

The three small dots appear at the bottom of the message thread. They disappear momentarily before a video appears. Against my better judgment, I hit play.

It's Aria out at the bar we were at last night. It's a lot busier tonight. Fridays always are; the live band draws a crowd, and the dance floor should be packed. She holds the phone out far enough that I can see the black lace top she is wearing and that the faces of the men around her are far too close. The music plays as the three of them continue to dance, two sets of hands sliding all over her body before one of the men pulls her into a kiss. The video cuts off there, leaving the picture of her kissing another man as the final frame.

Before I can think better of it, I'm out of my chair, my

phone to my ear as I start demanding she answers her fucking phone under my breath. I grab my keys off the table near the door and, within seconds, I'm in my car heading to the bar. If she wants to play this game, I'll play.

But I play to win.

CHAPTER
Four

ARIA

I pull out of the kiss to hit send. If Theo is going to ignore me, then I'm going to have some fun.

"I need a drink," I shout at what's-his-name in front of me. He looks over my shoulder at the guy I'm grinding on behind me, and they share a look before he heads to the bar.

We keep dancing until his friend comes back with 3 shots in hand. I'm handed one of the plastic cups of clear liquid. Immediately, I place the cup to my lips and knock it back. The burn of tequila stings my throat as I raise my hand above my head, like somehow it would take away the burn.

The boys just laugh as they take their shots without even the slightest flinch. The one behind me, I think his name is Chase, starts kissing my neck. Resting my head against his shoulder, I reach out to the blonde one, pulling him back into me. I can't even blame the tequila for not knowing his name; I just didn't give a fuck when they approached me. There is no need for names when I won't see them again after tonight. It's not like I can moan out his name while his friend's dick is in my mouth.

I turn my face toward Chase, or is his name Chance? Either way, I pull his lips onto mine as I guide his friend's hand up my shirt. Chad's hands grip my waist, pulling me back into him, feeling his cock harden through his jeans. My fingers slide up into the dirty blonde hair of the man in front of me. His hand meets mine at the back of his neck. He begins guiding my hand down his chest, then his abs, until he's sliding my hand down his pants. He places my hand on top of his dick. I rub my thumb gently over his tip, smearing the drops of precum around his rock-hard cock. His head falls back with a devious smile.

"Do you boys want to get out of here?" I ask over the music. But before they have a chance to answer, a strong, tattooed hand grips my wrist and pulls my hand out of this guy's pants. Anger flashes across the guy's face before it morphs into terror. Chaz almost immediately backs off of me. I turn to see Theo staring daggers at the men.

I pull my hand from his grip and laugh, "Now you want my attention? Too late, I've moved on." I look back to the guys I was dancing with, but they both back away as Theo barks out demands at them.

"No," I say, standing my ground.

"No, what?" He says, stepping closer to me. I'm forced to look up to keep eye contact.

"I'm not leaving."

"Now you can walk out of here on your own, or I will carry you out. Either way, we are leaving." I try to take a step back when his hands grip my waist and I'm thrown over his shoulder. He pushes through the crowd to the entrance.

Once we make it out the front doors, he places me down. Before I have a chance to argue, his hand is on the small of my back as he guides me to a black car still running directly in front of the entrance doors. He opens the passenger door and motions for me to sit. Once I'm seated, he shuts the door and walks around the front of the car, handing the valet what must be a few hundred dollars. I bet the only cash this man carries is hundreds with the way he tips.

Once seated behind the wheel and his door is shut, I turn toward him, "What the fuck was -"

"Seatbelt." He interrupts.

I stare at him, not comprehending what he's saying. He looks over to me, "Put on your seatbelt," he demands quietly.

I flop back into the seat and put on the seat belt. The buckle clicks into place.

"Good girl."

He turns and looks out the windshield before speeding out of the parking lot. The rush has me feeling a little dizzy.

"Now, are you going to tell me why you stormed off last night, ignored me all day today, and then proceeded to win the gold medal in cockblocking tonight?"

With one eyebrow raised, he looks over to me, "Gold medal in cockblocking?" The corners of his lip tug upwards before returning to look at the road.

"Yeah, I was about to be fucked by a couple of men I met at the bar since the person I wanted to fuck wouldn't answer my messages." I don't know why he thinks he can ignore me all day, give me no answers, and still have the right to swoop in and make demands. He has done nothing to earn my respect, let alone submission.

Yet I listen.

"It would take two random men to simultaneously fuck you to equate to what we did in the bathroom last night?" He turns his smile toward me as he beams with pride. Cocky motherfucker.

"They could try." I start feeling a buzz, but try and remember how much I actually drank. I wasn't at the bar that long. I ordered myself a beer when I got there and then had the shot that what's-his-name bought. I should not be this buzzed. Honestly, I shouldn't be buzzed at all.

"You still haven't answered my questions."

"Purposefully." His smile is gone as he focuses back on the road.

"Why? What did my mom say that had you running for the hills?" In her drunken state, it could have been anything. She probably hit on him and made a scene when he rejected her. She craves acceptance and probably figured she had a shot with a man who didn't know her past. Then, when he rejected her passes, she got all offended and aggressive. A scenario that happens often enough, I can probably quote the conversation. Usually, I don't give a fuck about what is going on in her love life. I have been caught up in enough of her drama my entire life, so I know to steer clear. But this time it's affecting mine.

"I take it your mom didn't give you any answers last night?"

"Nope, she passed out on the drive home. And I was out of the house before she woke up today. Not like she would have told me anyway," I lean my head against the cold window.

"What about your dad?"

"Dead."

His head shoots to me briefly, before focusing back on the road. His fists are gripping the steering wheel tighter. I rest my head back on the window, my eyelids getting heavier.

"I hadn't heard Luke died. I'm sorry."

"No. Luke is fine, last I heard. Do you know him?"

He looks over to me with confusion blanketing his face, "Luke isn't your father?"

"Nope, I found out at my ninth birthday party when he got the results of an at-home DNA test. Happy Birthday to me. I lost the majority of my family. You knew them?" My words are starting to slow.

"Yeah, I knew both of them. Who is your dad?" A mixture of amusement and sympathy crosses his face.

"Some Guy named Jeremy Dodd. He died six or seven years ago. I tried to find him when I turned eighteen, but he was already dead." I relax back into the leather seat. If he wasn't going to fuck me because of whatever my mother told him, he isn't going to fuck me now that he knows at least part of my traumatic backstory.

"I answered all your questions. Can you please answer some of mine? It's only fair." My words slurred. Why am I so exhausted?

"Baby, how much did you drink tonight?" He asks with what seems like concern.

"I'm 'Baby' again?" A smile forms on my lips hearing the endearment.

"Aria." He says more sternly.

"Just a beer and a shot," I yawn.

"Shit." His hand reaches over to me, gripping my chin, making me look at him. I smile, looking into his blue eyes before the world goes dark.

CHAPTER
Five

THEO

Aria is passed out in my front seat. If what she says is true and only had 2 drinks, something is wrong. Last night we had three or four before fucking, and she wasn't even buzzed. One shot should not be affecting her like this. Which means one of those assholes spiked her drink. I want to turn this car around and go back in there and rip their throats out, but I can't leave Aria unattended.

I open my phone and call Eddy.

"Shaw." He quickly answers the phone.

"Eddy, it's me. I need some help."

"What's up?" I can always count on Eddy, no matter if it's a work project or hiding a body, he's always down to help.

"I need a doc sent to my hotel room."

"For you?"

"No, I ran back into the girl from last night, but I think she's been roofied."

"So I'm taking it you're not the one who drugged her." He

laughs. In our line of work, drugs are easy to come by and used often on a job, but we never use them otherwise.

"I don't need to drug women to want to sleep with me. Especially ones who have been texting me all day begging for my cock."

"Was she really?" He laughs.

"Yeah."

"So why was she out with another man if she wanted to fuck you?" I can hear the keys click as he types on his computer.

"Men. Plural. She baited me out to the bar by flaunting two other men in front of me."

"Fuck, man, she sounds like a handful. Why were you ghosting her?"

"How do you know I was ghosting her?"

"Because you like them a little messy. So something happened for you not to be wrapped around her finger. Well, you did kidnap her from the club, so it seems, no matter the reason, you are wrapped around her finger." He mocks.

"I'm not." The words coming out in a growl.

"You're taking her home, aren't you?"

"Where else am I supposed to take her? I'm not taking her back to her mom's house."

"Well, there is an ER out there, isn't there? But, instead, you're taking her back to your place and having a private doctor come take care of her. Seems like you are. Why won't you take her to her mom?"

"It's Alana."

"Wait! T-the girl from last night is Alana? What the actual fuck, man?"

"No, it's worse. The girl from last night is Alana's daughter. Her twenty-two-year-old daughter."

"Wait, you are back in town for less than twenty-four hours, and you end up hooking up with the girl your ex-fiancé tried to pass off as your daughter."

"Yeah, so you see why I tried to ghost?"

"Fuck you really do like them messy. Fetterman is on his way to the penthouse. How far out are you?"

"Pulling into the parking garage now."

"Ok, get your girl upstairs. I'll let the front desk know to expect him and send him up."

"Thanks, man." The call ends, and I look over to Aria, who is still passed out against the window.

After carefully getting her out of the car and upstairs, I place her gently on my bed. Moments later, there's a knock on the door. Letting the doctor in, I guide him back to the main bedroom.

"She was dancing for maybe an hour. Before she passed out, she said she only ordered one beer and was given one shot. And I know she has a way higher alcohol tolerance."

He raises an eyebrow at me but doesn't ask any further questions. A perk of having money is the privacy. "How long ago do we suspect she was drugged?"

"Forty minutes, an hour?" She was perfectly fine in the video she sent me, so she had to have been drugged after that.

"Do you believe her account of how much she drank?" I don't know what he is trying to imply.

"Yes. She had no reason to lie to me, and when I got there to pick her up, she was completely fine." Defensiveness rises in my voice. I don't know why I am so protective over a random girl I met in a bar last night. But she isn't just a random girl. There is a shared history, whether she knows it or not. It's a history that can't get romantically entangled.

"Well, I will need to pump her stomach and then give her some fluids. She is going to feel like shit tomorrow, but her vitals seem stable, so it doesn't look like she will OD." He rambles off a few more things before asking me to help her into the shower.

"The easiest way to pump her stomach is just to make her puke, and it will be an easier clean-up in the shower than your bed." The doc goes to sit her up, but I get in his way and pick her up myself.

I place her on one end of the walk-in shower, propped up against the tile wall. As the doc starts giving her the meds, I walk into my room and pull out one of my t-shirts and a pair of sweats. By the time I am back in the bathroom, Aria is puking. The doctor rolls his eyes and starts muttering.

"If doing your job is an issue, I am sure I can reach out to the council and discuss your removal." Normally, I wouldn't dare speak to anyone like this, but I can see the pawn tattoo peeking out under his rolled-up sleeve. I outrank this mother-fucker, and I will not let him disrespect me or my guest. He quickly changes his demeanor.

Once Aria has emptied the entire content of her stomach, her eyes flutter open momentarily before closing again. The doctor goes to remove her soiled clothes, and she lets out a weak groan and attempts to pull away.

"Stop," I demand. Aria may not be fully conscious, but she is aware enough to express her discomfort. Tonight has been traumatizing enough; let's not add a stranger undressing her without her consent to the list. "I will handle her from here. Why don't you go get set up for the IV, and I'll bring her out when she is ready?"

"Why did you call a doctor if you were just going to dictate everything that needed to be done? Why are you wasting my time?" He needs to check his attitude before he pisses off the wrong man.

"I called you to take care of her, not to undress her without her consent." I bark at him. "Now go do your job, then get out," I slam the door in his face before he has a chance to move.

I walk back over to Aria, who has her eyes closed and her head resting against the tile wall.

"Hey Baby, can you hear me?" I kneel down next to her.

"Mmm." She says softly.

"You have had a rough night and have puke on your clothes. You need to get cleaned up. Can I help you?" She nods slightly.

"I'm going to turn the water on so it can warm up while we get you undressed," I explain as I walk to the other side of the shower and start the water. I don't know how much of this she will remember, but my focus right now is that she is aware of everything being done around her. The water warms up pretty quickly, and the shower begins to fill with steam.

"I'm going to start removing your clothes. If you want me to stop, I'll stop, just let me know when. Can you do that for me?" Her head nods gently. I carefully start removing her other clothes, narrating as I go.

Once she's naked, I take her to the other side of the shower, grab the handle of the shower head to lower it, and start rinsing her off. She has become slightly more aware but is still fairly out of it. She doesn't fight me, but I repeatedly check in and make sure she is ok with everything that I'm doing.

Once clean, I turn the water off and carry her out of the shower. I rest her body against my chest as I wrap her in a towel.

"Baby, I need your help. I need to sit you up so I can help get you dressed. Think you can do that for me?" She nods her head a little more forcefully than before.

She's still weak and exhausted, but the drugs seem to not be affecting her as much. Hopefully, this means after some fluids, she will rest up and not have too many issues tomorrow.

I sit her on the toilet and begin toweling off her body. With one hand still on her, I reach to the counter and grab the clothes. I place the t-shirt over her head and pull it down, covering the majority of the exposed skin. Once she is fully dressed, I lift her back up. This time she wraps her arms around my neck, which I take as another good sign.

The doctor has his setup ready and is looking at his phone when I walk past him. I place Aria down on the bed and start to move out of the doctor's way when her hand reaches for my arm. "Please, don't." Her whisper hoarse.

I squeeze her hand gently, "I'm not going anywhere, Baby Girl." I rest her hand down before walking to the other side of the bed and climbing in next to her.

With one arm wrapped around her and the other holding her free hand, the doctor starts the IV. Her body tenses, and a small tear falls softly down her cheek.

"You're doing such a great job, Aria. We're almost done, and then you can just get some rest." Her hand tightens around mine.

After about twenty minutes, the bag of fluids is empty, so the doctor removes her IV. He bandages her arm and then leaves in a huff. I don't walk him out; instead, I debate on telling Eddy that I never want him allowed near Aria or me ever again. I sit holding Aria's hand until she falls asleep. Once I'm confident she's out for the night, I slide out of bed and take one of the pillows out to the couch.

I try to grab some sleep before having to explain everything that happened to her tomorrow.

CHAPTER
Six

ARIA

I stretch my arms over my head, noting the tightness in my muscles. I run my fists over my eyes, opening them to see I'm alone in a room that's not my own. Blackout curtains are pulled closed, letting just a sliver of light through the window. Sitting up, I look around, trying to get an idea of who I went home with last night. I try to think back, and the last thing I can remember is dancing at the bar. The unease of not being able to remember sets in as I note a lack of any personal touches in the room. No photos hanging on the walls to jog my memory, nothing left out on any of the furniture, and nothing seemingly out of place. Just what appears to be a large window and two doors. Standing, I feel the heaviness of the clothes as they hang off my body. It only takes me one step to feel the world spin. I find my grounding and walk to the door. I'm hoping this leads to a bathroom. My hand never breaks contact with a wall as I enter the room and search for a light switch.

The lights flash on, allowing me to see my reflection for the first time. My eyes are sunken in, and my skin is pale. I stare at the reflection of a lifeless portrayal of myself, scanning down my body, my attention is immediately pulled to my arm. It's wrapped as though I donated blood. Did I get an IV? I quickly splash water on my face and rinse out my mouth, trying to wake myself up, before I try to sneak out. I was alone in bed, so whoever owns this home may not even be here. One can hope.

I step out of the bathroom, letting the light flood into the bedroom. I find the light switch and flip it on. The light helps me see that while I have my shoes tucked up by the bed, none of my clothes are anywhere to be seen. I try to remember what I was wearing last night, jeans and a T-shirt, maybe. If I can't remember, they aren't that important, and I can abandon them here if need be. I grab my shoes and head toward the door, pulling it open slowly. I start to peek through the crack as it opens, into what I think is the living room. The floor-to-ceiling windows continue across the entire apartment, looking out over the city skyline. The furniture is sleek and minimal, but easily some of the nicest quality I've seen.

I look around to see if there are any personal touches out here, but nothing gives me any indication of who lives here. Whoever it is has money. I freeze in my steps, *Theo.*

A moment later, the front door opens. I try to inch back so he doesn't see me, but within just a few steps, Theo is standing in front of me.

"Good to see you awake," He says with a sly smile on his lips. He is holding a couple of bags and 2 coffee cups. He places all but one of the coffees down on the kitchen island before walking over to me. I can't help but watch the way he walks in his gray sweatpants. His free hand gently lifts and brushes a stray strand of hair behind my ear before offering me the cup. I hold the warm liquid in my hands as I look up at him. This doesn't make sense. He ghosted me. There is no way he was the guy I was dancing with last night.

Why do I not remember? I don't ever get blackout drunk, not for the lack of trying. What happened?

Nothing is making sense. My thoughts swirl as my chest tightens. I look around for anything that can answer my questions, but nothing is giving me any information.

What happened at the club?

Why can't I remember?

Why am I at Theo's?

What did I do?

It becomes harder to breathe.

"What-?" is all I can manage between labored breaths.

"Aria." His tone, calm. He gently places his hand on my cheek, guiding me to look at him. I squeeze my eyes shut, trying to calm my breathing, but it's not helping.

"Aria, look at me." He commands gently. At that moment, my body urges me to trust him, so I obey. I open my eyes and look at him. His gaze intently on me, not out of anger but concern.

"Take one deep breath, in through your nose, out your mouth." My body instantly follows his direction. "That's my girl. Again."

We go through the steps a few more times until it doesn't feel like my heart is going to beat out of my chest. Our eyes never break contact.

"You are safe. You are ok." His thumb caresses my cheek.

"What happened to me?" Tears well up in my eyes, a few cascading down my face.

He pulls me into his chest, one hand cradling my head, and the other around my back, pulling me in close. The embrace triggers even more tears to fall.

He holds me and lets me cry for several minutes. As soon as I catch my breath and start to pull away. The hand he had wrapped around my back drops to my arm, and then my hand.

He gently pulls me toward the couch. I sit on the far side and curl up between the back and the arm. He hands me the blanket that was strewn across the couch and throws a pillow to the other chair.

Did he sleep out here? I pull the blanket up over my body and realize it smells like him. I do not understand why my body has the reaction it does. This man has a dirty mouth and a huge cock, who defiled me in a bar bathroom. Why is he being comforting? Why does the smell of him relax me?

What the actual fuck is happening?

"What is the last thing you remember?" He asks cautiously.

"You ghosted me, so I went to The Saddle to dance, but after that, nothing." He looks like he is choosing his words very carefully.

"You sent me a video of you dancing with two men." His words don't sound angry, but the look in his eyes tells me otherwise. Heat rushes to my cheeks. It sounds like something I would do, but it feels weird being called out for it.

"Sorry," I whisper, almost embarrassed.

He swallows hard before saying through gritted teeth, "You have nothing to be sorry for. You are allowed to live your life and have fun. I do not get a say in how you live your life or judge your decisions when I was the one ignoring you."

"How did I end up here?" I still don't understand what happened.

"I showed up at the bar and pulled you off the dance floor. Once you were in my car, you started to complain about being dizzy and tired. I questioned you on how much you drank since it was still pretty early in the night. You told me you had only had 2 drinks. Which made me suspect something was put in one of your drinks. My suspicions were confirmed when you passed out in my car before getting here." I try to hear every word he is saying, but my mind keeps replaying.

Something was put in your drink.

What is he saying?

Was I drugged?

Who did this?

Who was I with?

What were they going to do?

What did they do?

What did Theo do?

I curl back into myself and feel the chest tightness returning.

"I called a doctor who took care of you. He had you puke to get as much of the drug out of your system and IV to help fight off the hangover-like symptoms today."

I look at Theo and breathe the way he instructed me earlier.

"I think they slipped something in your drink right before I got there. They didn't have enough time to follow through with whatever their plan was. He pauses, "And once you were here, you immediately got help from the doctor, and then I cleaned you up and put you to bed, alone."

The last word gives me both relief and disappointment. The entire reason I kept messaging Theo was because I wanted to see him again and fuck him again. And the thought of him being in complete control, using me however he needed to get his satisfaction, is kind of hot.

God, how fucked up does that make me?

"What are you thinking, Baby?"

My face immediately heats. I throw the blanket down and go to stand, "Nothing, just going to add last night to the never-ending list of fucked up shit that has happened to me." I try to brush this off. He has dealt with enough of my baggage. I try to find my shoes and phone, I'll call a ride downstairs. "Thanks for all the help, but I'm going to-"

He grabs my shoulder, pulling me back to him.

"Aria, do not lie to me." He breathes against my lips. I move my gaze from his lips to his eyes. A fire burns behind them. My core tightens as his hand moves from my shoulder to my face, "Tell me what you were thinking." He almost groans.

Part of me wants to tell him. Part of me wants to do whatever this man says. The other part wants to see what will happen if I tell him no. Will he give up? Will he teach me why I should listen?

I smile as I look him in the eye, "Make me."

His eyes darken before he looks away, letting out an amused growl.

He mumbles "Fuck it" before returning his gaze to me.

"Are you sure about that, Baby? Because I can and I will." He taunts.

"Oh really?" I question, egging him on.

"Really." The amusement tints his voice.

"Prove it." His hand quickly slides from my cheek to my throat, gently pressing on the sides.

My eyes stay locked on his, a smile forms on my lips. I drop my head and rest into his hold.

"So are you going to tell me what you were thinking, or am I going to have to show you what happens when you do not listen?"

"Which ends with me cumming on your cock?" He lets out a sultry laugh.

"Is that what you want, Baby Girl? "

I nod my head, "Yes, please."

"Then, tell me what you were thinking." He says slowly, pausing between words.

I swallow hard as I find the words to say.

"I was disappointed."

"About?" He encourages me, his hand still around my throat, holding my face in front of his.

"That when you brought me home last night, you didn't use me." I close my eyes, waiting for him to pull away. But he doesn't.

"Look at me." He commands softly. I immediately obey. His eyes are focused on mine. Where I expected to see pity or concern, I see lust.

"What did you want me to do to you?" He quietly prompts.

"I wanted you to use me however you needed to be satisfied." His eyes darken.

"Would you like me to use you now?"

I nod my head in response, bringing a smirk to his face.

"Are you familiar with stoplights?" I nod. I look at him with confusion. Why the hell am I answering driver's ed questions?

"Green means go, yellow means proceed with caution, and red means stop. If you are ever uncomfortable with what I am doing, you will give me a color and let me know. Do you understand?" I nod. "Good girl."

He drops his hand from my throat. I immediately miss his touch. He brushes his dark hair out of his face before picking me up and throwing me over his shoulder. I can't help but giggle before his hand smacks my ass, hard, causing me to gasp.

"That's more like it." He teases. He walks into the bedroom and puts me down at the foot of the bed. He turns and closes the door. I watch him as he walks around the bed to the closet, he reaches in to grab something before climbing onto the bed. He sits in the center against the headboard, watching me. His look alone is sending lightning to my core. He's not even touching me, and I can feel the wetness between my legs.

"Strip." He commands. My body instantly reacts and begins to pull his shirt off of me. It falls to the floor near my feet. I watch him look over my body as I drop his sweatpants around my ankles and step out of them, leaving me bare and vulnerable.

He slides his sweats off his waist and slowly kicks them off.

"Crawl to me."

I do as he says, climbing onto the bed and crawling toward him. Seeing the way he enjoys the control he has over me has my heart racing. I smile as he stops me when I reach his waist. His cock is hard and directly below my face. I can't help but lick my lips, hoping he will let me taste him.

"Such a greedy little slut." My core tightens at his words. If anyone else called me a slut, everything would hard stop. I don't care if I'm seconds away from cumming, we would be done. But somehow when Theo says it, it's almost endearing. When Theo says it, I want to be a slut. *His slut.*

"Go ahead. Choke on my cock."

I immediately take him to the back of my throat. I bob my head up and down a few times, coating his dick in my spit, before grabbing him at the base and twisting. I wrap my lips around his tip and suck.

He lets out a breathy moan, encouraging me to continue. He threads his fingers in my hair, holding my head in place. He begins to thrust his hips, driving his cock deep into my throat. Tears begin to collect on my face, mixing with the drool pooling at the base of his dick.

"You look so beautiful with my cock in your mouth." He pulses a few more times before holding me down and forcing his cock as far as it would go.

I try to swallow around his tip, earning me a "*fucccckkkk.*" as he cums. He releases my head, and I slowly pull him out of my mouth, making sure I have taken every drop of him.

He adjusts in his seat for just a moment before his focus is back on me.

"Lay back, legs open. Show me how you touch that pretty pussy of yours."

I sit back and spread my legs, sliding my fingers down my body until my fingers glide through my arousal. I slowly press my two fingers inside myself, coating them fully. I watch as Theo's gaze drops from my eyes to my cunt. One of his hands grips his cock, the other is gently brushing his lips. I pull my fingers out and slide them until I'm rubbing my clit. My fingers press gentle circles as my body begins to tighten. I bring my free hand to my breast and begin to pinch my nipple, adding to the heat inside my core.

Theo's eyes darken. "Did I say you could touch anything other than your pussy?"

"No," I say breathlessly, dropping my hand.

"Good girl. The next time you do something like that, there will be punishment."

I take a deep inhale at his words. Being called a good girl already had me wanting to cum, but hearing about his punishments has me melting. A smirk forms on my face as I watch his eyes follow my hand as it returns to my nipple.

"Aria..." He warns. But I pull harder, throwing my head back at the sting. Moments later, there is a hand around my throat, forcing me to look at him.

"Trying to push the boundaries, are we? If you can't keep your hands where they belong, you don't get to use them anymore." I watch as he pulls me to the top of the bed. Wrapping my hands in a black tie before tying them to the headboard. I wiggle my wrists to see if I can pull them free, but it only makes them tighter. I look over my shoulder to see Theo kneeling behind me. He grabs my waist and pulls me back to him, forcing me into a bent-over position in front of him.

"You look so good when you're bent over in front of me."

He says as he slaps my ass, causing a tingling sensation in my core. I let out a soft moan, dropping my head between my arms.

He grips my hair at the base of my neck before pulling my head back. "Now you're going to take my cock until I'm finished with you."

"Use me." I plead, "Please." I gasp as he thrusts himself inside me, hard. Our bodies pound against each other repeatedly as he continues to move inside me. His grip on my waist tightens, digging into my skin. I breathe through the hint of pain that is causing my pussy to clench around his cock. He groans before smacking my ass again, causing me to arch back into him at the sting. My muscles begin to spasm in my shoulders, from the strain I'm putting on them, but having him fully in control makes this whole scene so much hotter. I can't pull away; I am at his mercy. He is fucking me for his pleasure, not mine. Which weirdly is getting me off. My body stiffens as he slows down his pace. My body shutters with every pulse inside me.

"God, yes." I breathe out as I can feel his dick twitch inside me. He thrusts deep into me one more time before finding his release.

He slowly pulls out and kisses my back.

He unties the knot around my wrist, and the return of blood flow causes my fingers to tingle. I start flexing and rotating my wrists, as he guides my body against his.

"Hands feel ok?" He asks gently, his hands sliding down my arms. He gently grabs my wrists and inspects them for injuries.

"Yeah, just tingly. But they are good." I answer hesitantly. My wrists are sore, along with my shoulders, but I don't want him to think I can't handle this. I love everything we just did, and I want to be able to explore this more with him. He took part of me I was ashamed to admit existed and began exploring it with me safely. If I tell him I'm anything less than perfect, he won't do it again.

"Aria, talk to me. What's going on in the gorgeous little head of yours?" He says as he pulls me down into his lap. His arms wrap around me. "Tell me what's going on so I can help."

He gently brushes my hair out of my face.

"My body is sore." I begrudgingly whisper.

"Is that it?" He kisses my neck as he slides his hands to my shoulders. He digs gently, massaging out some of the knots.

"Yeah. I don't want you to think I can't handle this." His hands pause for a moment before moving lower down my back. The pressure causes slight discomfort, but the second he releases, my muscles begin to relax.

"Thank you for being honest with me." My body tenses waiting for the rejection. At this point in my life, I should be immune to the hurt of rejection. The fact that it has happened time and time again shows that something about me is the problem. "But I need you to trust me. If something is ever too much, you need to tell me. I don't want to push you past your limits and hurt you mentally or physically."

I look back at him, trying to see if he's just saying this to be nice, but he seems to mean it.

"I can stay?" Now he looks at me, confused.

"Why wouldn't you be able to?" He places his hands on my face, holding my gaze on his face.

"I don't know." He kisses my forehead before releasing my face. He seems to know there is more, but he isn't going to pry.

"Do you want to go take a shower, and I'll make some lunch? We can talk more once you're fed."

I nod as he gently releases me. He walks into the bathroom, starts the water, and places a clean towel on the counter. He disappears into what I assume is his closet before standing back in front of the vanity in a new pair of sweats and placing what looks like sweats and a t-shirt onto the bathroom counter.

"Water should be warm enough. I pulled some clean clothes for you since yours are not back yet from the dry cleaner." He walks back in front of me before kissing the top of my head, "Do you need anything else before I go get food ready?"

"Why did you ghost?" The words fall out of my mouth before I can think about it. He looks up to the ceiling before returning his gaze to mine.

"I promise I will explain everything, but let's get you cleaned up and fed first."

My eyes look to the ground as he kisses the top of my head one last time before he walks away. The door closes quietly, and I walk into the steam-filled bathroom.

CHAPTER
Seven

THEO

I close the oven door and set the timer before heading back to the fridge. Grabbing the last of my fruits and yogurt I have, I take it over to the counter, making a note that I need to order more groceries. The lawyers still haven't responded to my emails. With how long he has been taking between emails, I am expecting to be here at least another week. I throw all the food I just grabbed into the blender along with some protein milk. I hit the pulse button, mixing everything into a smoothie. I don't know when the last time Aria ate was, so I want to make sure she has something healthy in her system, so we can avoid a huge drop.

A hand on my arm startles me as I look over to see Aria next to me. She must have walked in while the blender was going. I finish pouring the smoothie into the cup before handing it to her.

"Drink." I instruct. She listens and then sits on the barstool next to the counter.

"So are you finally going to answer my questions?" She takes another sip of the smoothie. "And thanks."

"You're welcome." I start rinsing some of the dishes, "And yes. I'll answer all of your questions." I turn off the water and dry my hands on the black hand towel next to my sink. I lean back against the counter before tossing the towel aside.

"What do you want to know first?"

"Why were you trying to ghost me?"

"I thought it was best to put some distance between us."

"Cool, not what I asked." My eyes flicker to hers, an amused smirk on my lips.

"Outside of the club, when I saw your mom-"

"You realized the age gap, and it scared you away."

"Are you going to keep interrupting?" I can't help but let out a soft chuckle. She is a feisty one.

"Are you going to keep beating around the bush?" My hand flexes. What I would give to bend her over this counter and show her exactly how that attitude of hers makes me feel.

"Give me a chance." She shuts her mouth before taking another drink of the smoothie. "When I saw your mom, I was extremely angry. And it's for the same reason I distanced myself." I pause for a minute, bracing myself for what I am about to say. "Your mother and I were engaged 22 years ago."

Her eyes widen, and I can almost see the gears turning inside her mind. Her eyes flick down to the counter before returning to mine, then back down to the counter. She is silent for several moments.

She finally looks back to me, "And we are a hundred percent certain you are not my dad?"

My stomach twists.

"I took a paternity test, stating there was no possibility of me being the biological father. It was the reason I broke the engagement off with your mom." I take a breath, also remembering what she said in the car last night. "You also had mentioned you took a test and were told a guy named Jeremy Dodd was your father."

"Right." She breathes a sigh of relief, and her body begins to relax.

"Yeah," she swallows, "that's why Luke left." She sits quiet another moment, and I give her time to process.

"How many men was my mom fucking?" It's not a question of disbelief, but disappointment. Whatever little sliver of respect Aria had left of her mother is gone.

"I was only aware of her having slept with Luke, so at least three?"

"No wonder everyone hated me! I was the epitome of an 'affair baby'! What the actual fuck?" I let her vent, knowing if she kept it all inside, it would destroy her. It damn near killed me, and I didn't have to grow up under the umbrella of scrutiny. She has every right to be angry.

She starts to calm down and returns to the kitchen island.

"Did you love her?" She asks. The question taking me back. This was not what I was expecting.

"We started dating right out of high school. Stayed together through my college years. I stayed close to home instead of going to my first choice to stay close to her. When she told me she was pregnant, it was a surprise, but I was excited to start that new phase of my life. It just seemed like the natural next step. When I found out she had been cheating, the dream life for us turned into a nightmare. Even if the baby, you, were mine, I couldn't imagine spending the rest of my life not being able to trust the person I was with. I was willing to fight to get custody, but you weren't mine, so I left, cut ties completely. Went and took a job that provided me with the life I have now." She takes in every word.

"Why didn't you find a housewife to give you kids, if that's what you wanted?"

"I had trust issues after that. And it wasn't fair to get with someone and then not be able to trust them based on what someone else did. Until I found someone I could trust without question, I didn't want it anymore."

"Do you think you will ever want it?" She asks cautiously.

"Why is that question making you nervous?"

"Why are you answering a question with another question?" I smile as she proves she is still her sassy self, even after this confession.

"I'm not sure, I'm already forty-four. Most men my age who have kids have teenagers already. If I get someone pregnant today, I will be sixty-two at the kid's graduation."

"So no?" Her gaze drops again.

"So I'm not sure." I place my hand under her chin and lift her gaze to mine."Baby, why do you ask?"

"No reason." She looks away.

"Aria." Her eyes snap back to mine.

She sighs before responding, "I just haven't decided if I want kids someday, and the idea of dating someone who doesn't want them, and then not getting a choice is sad."

She pauses before realizing what she was implying, "Shit, not that I'm thinking we're going to fall madly in love and have kids one day." She breathes again before getting flustered again. "Shit. Not that I don't think we could, I'm just not thinking we will." I let her ramble on for a little longer before I interrupt her.

"Baby, it's smart of you to be thinking like that at your age. If you know, one way or another, what you want, then you need to find someone who wants that too. But you are young and have plenty of time to figure that out."

The tension in her body starts to release again. "And I

would love to explore this more, but I also know the odds of this being a lasting thing are slim." She looks at me, slightly offended. "It's nothing against you, but we live in different states. There is a twenty-year age gap; you're just starting your life, and I'm pretty settled in mine. There's the whole 'your family hates me thing'."

"Well, the only 'family' you speak of is my mom, and I hate her too. So you can cross that worry off your list." She takes another drink of the smoothie, reminding me of the pizza in the oven.

I stand and walk over to the oven, as my phone rings. Pulling it out of my pocket, I see it's finally the lawyers.

"Aria, can you come pull the pizza out of the oven? I need to take this call." She nods before standing and walking over to the stove.

"It's Reeves, and you better have answers."

CHAPTER
Eight

ARIA

    Theo walked towards a room on the other side of the apartment. His work voice is very different from the way he speaks to me. Just the tone shift alone was intimidating. I look around the kitchen for a potholder but settle on a dish towel folded a couple of times. I pull the pizza out of the oven just as the timer goes off. While it begins to cool on the stovetop I start rummaging through the kitchen drawer trying to find a pizza cutter or any knife, really. This kitchen is stocked, but barely. There is no way anyone lives here full-time. Theo definitely doesn't. I wonder if he just rented it out while he is in town or if he owns it. But why would he own it? He hasn't been back for two decades. If he does own this place maybe I can offer to apartment-sit while he is out of town. Anything so I don't have to go back to my mom's. Like if this place is going to sit empty anyway. I find the steak knives, pull one out, and begin cutting the pizza into slices.

    A door closes in the direction Theo had gone. A moment later, he is standing behind me with his chest against my back.

"Thank you." He says as he presses his lips to the top of my head, "Sorry about that, the lawyers finally got back to me."

"What lawyers?" I ask as I finish the last slice across the pizza.

"I'm back in town dealing with finalizing everything from my mother's estate. And the lawyer she was using is useless." He reaches into the cupboard to the right of us and pulls out two plates.

"Her estate, like real estate?"

"Kind of, it's all of her property and belongings." It's then that I realize what he means.

I spin around within his grasp and look up to him.

"I'm so sorry." He chuckles a little before kissing my forehead.

"It's ok Baby, She passed away last year. The lawyer is just incompetent and has been dragging this all out way longer than it needs to be."

"Still, She is your mom," I say conflicted. I know I wouldn't give two shits if it was my mom but most people have better relationships with their parents than I do.

"I appreciate the concern, but I am ok." I turn back to the stove and place a slice on his plate before putting a slice on mine.

"Did you figure everything out?" I ask with a mouth full of stuffed crust.

"Do you always eat pizza backwards?" He laughs.

"Only when the crust is stuffed. It's the best part." He smiles at me.

"That's not the only thing that's best when stuffed from the back." I roll my eyes, as he looks at me hungrily.

We sit on the couch as I take another bite, the melted cheese slightly burns my mouth, causing me to let out a gentle moan. A devious smirk crosses Theo's face.

"What now?"

"Nothing, just love hearing the noises you make." He chuckles while going to take a bite of his pizza.

He does, does he? Well, I can do him one better. I lean back and dangle the pizza above me. Slowly licking up the slice, cleaning all the sauce off the side. The second it touches my tongue I let out a sensual moan.

"Mmmm, that's *so* hot." Theo's eyes narrow as he watches me, "I don't know if I can fit the whole thing in my mouth, but I want it inside me *so bad*." He continues to watch as the grease from the pizza drips down my face. I let out another moan, this one louder as I push my chest out. Sliding the pizza into my mouth taking a slow and sensual bite, I swallow hard and watch Theo's gaze bounce between my throat and chest. Theo looks up to the ceiling before looking back at me.

"If that's how you want to play, let's play." He says as he begins to crawl on top of me.

"Whatever do you mean?" I play innocent as he pushes me back against the arm of the couch.

"Oh you know exactly what you were doing, and now you need to deal with the consequences of your actions."

"I'm just enjoying this pizza you were so gracious to make for me." I tease.

He pins me down to the couch, before taking the slice of pizza from my hand and putting it on the table.

"I wasn't done with that," I argue.

"It can wait." He kisses my neck, I immediately drop my head back giving him more space to kiss. Gently sliding one hand to the back of my neck, he pulls my lips to his. His mouth engulfs mine, parting my lips I tease him with my tongue. Pulling back for a moment, showing me the smile on his face.

"Strip." He commands and I immediately start sliding off the sweats he put me in. He pulls himself off me and yanks his shirt over his head, before sliding off his sweats. I take the brief moment of him not on me to pull off the t-shirt I am wearing. Theo slides me down the couch before kneeling next to the couch and putting my leg over his shoulder. He lowers his face to my cunt, licking up my center. Running my fingers through his hair, he palms my breast. My core tightens as he sucks my clit, causing my hips to buck against his face while his hand tightens around my thigh.

"Theo." I moan as the pressure builds in my core. My breath hitches as he slides 2 fingers inside me. He gently rubs his teeth against my clit eliciting a whimper from me.

He pulls back and looks at me, "You don't know what those sounds do to me, do you?"

"Show me." I beg.

Sliding one of my hands to his cock, I wrap my hand around it, feeling its pulse, "That's because of you." He praises, sending a shiver down my spine. My grip tightens as I start sliding my hand up and down his shaft causing him to let out a shuttered moan.

"Theo, fuck me." His eyes dart to mine and flood with need. The pressure in my core increases. He pulls his hips back, taking his dick from my hand before lining his hips at my entrance. The head of his cock, gently pressing inside me. Stretching around his size, I love the slight sting as he fully enters me.

"You feel so good, Baby." He groans. Hearing the way I am affecting him and seeing him on the verge of losing control because of me has my heart racing. He thrusts his hips slowly letting me feel every movement. My body trembles as he brushes my clit with his thumb. Lightning shoots through my core with every deep pump. The way he huffs with every thrust edges me closer to finishing. A whine is forced from my body, as my walls attempt to strangle his cock.

"Just like that baby." He encourages. My back arches off the couch as his thumb picks up speed and fire pools in my stomach.

"Theo." I moan, trying to tell him I'm about to cum but the words won't come out. My vision becomes fuzzy as the fire spreads under my skin.

"*Fucckkk.*" He moans. "You're doing such a good job Baby Girl."

"I- I- I can't." I stutter as my entire body is consumed by the shockwaves of my climax. My nails dig into his shoulders.

"Yes, you can Baby." He coaches, his hips unrelenting. His thumb continues to circle, sending wave after wave through my body. "You're taking it so well." He breathes against my neck.

Strangled noises exit my body instead of words, as he continues to fuck me recklessly.

His thrust slows momentarily, and my entire body tenses, my vision going dark. He plunges deep into me.

"Theo!" I scream as he spills himself inside me.

My body falls back onto the couch, my breathing heavy. My eyes are still closed as he lifts me against him. I rest my body against him as he walks us to the bedroom. He gently lays me down on the bed, before climbing in next to me.

"You're so beautiful when you're cumming on my dick." He whispers as he kisses my neck. A soft laugh comes from me as I roll over and position myself against his chest.

"My favorite place to be." I breathe, before falling asleep.

CHAPTER
Nine

ARIA

I listen for the shower to turn off, waiting for Theo to come back to bed. It is crazy how being drugged and essentially kidnaped less than 24 hours ago, I still feel more at peace in this practical stranger's house than I do at my mother's house. The woman who is supposed to love me more than anything in this world and protect me has been the one to harm me the most. All because I didn't share DNA with the man she had hoped I would. Weird if she hadn't fucked so many other men, I could be Theo's daughter. Luckily I get to be his Baby girl without actually being his child.

The sound of running water stops, so I look up from my phone to watch as Theo exits the shower. Something about water dripping down his tattooed abs has me wanting to go for a round two, or three, or whatever number we are on now. My phone starts buzzing and pulls my gaze away from the naked body I would much rather be licking at this very moment. The screen lights up, and the name that flashes across the screen gives me pause.

Mother dearest .

"Fuck." I groan.

"What's up?" Theo asks from the bathroom.

"My mother is calling," I answer. "I'm going to ignore it."

"She will call back until you answer, might as well just get it over with." He has a point. I reluctantly swipe my finger across the screen. I can hear her yelling even before the phone makes it to my ear.

"Where the fuck are you?" She screams.

"Does it matter?"

"So you went home with someone else last night? Trying for a new guy every night?" It's funny how she is trying to slut shame me when she of all people has no leg to stand on. I stifle a laugh but she must hear.

"What's so funny now, Aria? Trying to get a bingo on the std game board? You have become a whore, haven't you? Do you have no respect for me? Or yourself? Do you know what the people in this town say about you?"

"None of what they say about me is near as bad as what they say about you." I laugh, "Plus what they say about me is untrue or exaggerated, while everything they say about you is true."

"It is not!"

"If you say so."

"Come home now before any more rumors start!"

"Yeah, that's not going to happen. I'm going to stay right where I am."

"With how many men you have gone home with, do you even know this dick's name?"

"I do. You do too. If I'm not mistaken you wanted me to grow up calling him, what was it? Oh yeah, *Daddy*."

"What the fuck are you talking about?" She shouts.

"Now that I'm thinking about it, I think I will call him

Daddy." I catch Theo's heated gaze out of the corner of my eye. My core burns as his eyes are focused on me.

"Who are you talking about?" She shouts again. The fact she has no idea who I am talking about since there are so many options has me sick to my stomach.

"Goodbye Mom, I'll tell Theo you say hi." I quickly hang up the phone and then block my mother's contact, knowing that it is the only way I will have peace today.

Dropping my head back I sigh, fighting with my mom is so tiring. I need to get out of this town as soon as possible.

I look back over to Theo and he is standing in the exact same position he was a moment ago, the only difference is now his dick is hard.

My gaze flicks up to his face when he commands, "Come here."

I do as I am told, sliding out of the bed and walking until I am standing directly in front of him.

"Say that again."

"Say what again?" I ask.

"What did you just call me?" Confused, I look up at him.

"Baby, what did you just say to your mother? What did you say she wanted you to call me?"

"Daddy?" I watch as a smile forms on his lips.

"Again."

"*Daddy*," I stress each and every sound.

"Good girl." He brushes the hair out of my face before kissing me, hard. Running his tongue along my lips until I let him in.

Tossing his towel behind him onto the counter, he guides me into the shower, pressing me up against the glass as he turns the water back on.

Steam billows against the glass walls, engulfing us. His hands cup my face as kisses me again, more forcefully this time.

I kiss back, hanging on every kiss like it will be the last. He slides one hand down my body until he can place it between my legs. His fingers find the pool of wetness, as he presses against my entrance.

"You like calling me Daddy as much as I like to hear it don't you?" He smiles against my lips.

His fingers find my clit getting a breathy "Yes." in response. I gasp as he pinches my clit.

He brings his lips back down on my neck as his fingers begin to circle. I can't help but buck against his hand, wanting more pressure.

"Take what you need Baby Girl. " He encourages. "Ride me however you need."

His words send lightning down my spine.

"I want you inside me." I pant, wanting to cum around his cock.

"Turn around." He commands. I quickly do as I'm told. His hands grab my waist and pull me back into him. He presses down on my back forcing me into a bend in front of him. My hands brace against the glass, as my chest is pushed against the steam-filled wall. Theo slides his hand up my neck into my hair, grabbing a handful and pulling my head back. I smile as he takes control of me.

"I love how you want to be used by me." He moans as he pushes his dick inside me. I whimper as he pushes deeper, filling me with his length. Once he is fully seated inside he reaches his free hand around my body and traces my folds, sliding his fingers through my slickness. He continues to trace me until I buck against him as he grazes my clit. Pleasure shoots to my core. My hands flex against the glass as he repeats this motion, again and again. The pressure in my core slowly filling my body. Just when I think I am about to explode he removes his fingers and pulses his dick in and out of me. Each thrust pushes me closer and closer to combustion. He pulls my hair harder. The slight pain amplifies every feeling of pleasure. Heat spreads under my skin as he breathes against my neck, " You take my cock so well."

I moan as he thrusts harder, pressing me even further into the glass wall.

"Do you want to cum baby?"

"Yes." I breathe.

"Yes, who?" He pauses all motion.

"Yes Daddy, Please make me cum." I beg.

"Good girl." He immediately begins pounding inside me again, while teasing my clit. The sensation sending me over the edge. He groans as my pussy tightens around his cock. He jerks his hips. "Such a good girl." he rasps. His dick twitches inside me as he tries to hold in a groan emptying himself inside me.

I begin to stand off the glass as he pulls me to his chest.

"Perfect." He whispers, turning my head to look up at him. He gently presses his lips against mine. My eyes flutter closed as I rest into him. He gently pulls his hips back, pulling himself out of me. "Let's get cleaned up and then go lay back in bed."

I nod, finally feeling the exhaustion start creeping in.

CHAPTER
Ten

THEO

Aria lays asleep on my chest. I should be packing my things and getting ready to head back to the city. Apparently, once my lawyer got ahold of my mom's lawyer everything was done in a matter of minutes. Odd how a man who gets paid by the hour took his damn time filing this paperwork.

But things are really good right now with Aria. I know I didn't do anything wrong by leaving her mom, but I was the first man to abandon her. I can't do that again, especially now that I know how shitty Alana has been treating her. None of the shit she has had to deal with was her fault, yet as a child, she had to deal with all of it. I cannot leave her here to deal with it alone again.

"Hey Baby, I need you to wake up," I say softly next to her ear. She lets out a sleepy moan. Her body must be so tired, with everything I have put her through in the last couple of days.

"Yes, Daddy." My chest swells with pride at the endearment.

"I need to get packed before we leave."

"You're leaving?" The disappointment in her voice is enough to cement my decision to get her out of this town.

"Yeah, I'm headed back to the city. Don't worry Baby Girl, you're coming with me."

She looks at me confused.

"Do you have anything important that cannot be replaced at home? "

"Not really, I don't have anything sentimental if that's what you're asking."

"Good, send me a list of your sizes and necessities and I'll have what you need by the time we arrive."

"You're just going to buy me things instead of having me go home and pack them?" She laughs.

"Do you want to go home and deal with your mother?"

"New things it is." I smile.

"Your clothes from last night arrived while you were asleep, so if you would like to change into those, instead of traveling in my sweats, they are on the kitchen island."

"Thank you." She says as she starts pulling herself off the bed. I grab her wrist before she stands.

"Thank you, who?"

"Thank you, *Daddy.*" She smiles. I love that she loves this too. It's going to fucking suck when she moves on from this. But right here right now it's perfect. When she decides she needs something else, I'll support her but this, this right here is what I need. I watch as she walks into the kitchen the light shines off her naked silhouette.

I grab my phone to get everything set up.

"Its Shaw"

"Hey Eddie, I need a jet home, two passengers. "

"Two passengers? Is that a good idea?" He asks. I appreciate his concern but having every decision questioned is getting pretty old.

"Have I ever brought anyone home?"

"No."

"So it's a big deal that I am." I take a breath. "I have thought about this. Even if things don't work out with us, She deserves a better life, One she will not get here."

"I'm just making sure. You don't have a great history with relationships, but if you have thought this through, I'm not going to stop you. Just make sure you're prepared for the consequences of her finding out how you make your money."

"The worst that could happen is she leaves, and I know one day she will. I just can't leave her here. I thought Alana destroyed my life, it's nothing compared to what Aria has been going through."

"The jet will be ready in an hour. Need anything else?"

"Aria will need some things, I need you to have Mia start gathering them and having them at the penthouse. As soon as Aria sends me the list, I will send it to you."

"Can do. We will see you in a few hours."

I end the call as Aria walks back in, in the clothes I picked her up in the other night.

"Ready?" I ask, knowing that the only thing she owns in the apartment is her phone.

"I was thinking." She says slowly walking back towards me.

"What about?"

"I don't know if I want just anyone buying my necessities."

"Ok, go on." I grab her hand and pull her between my legs.

"All clothes fit so differently, so I'd like to be able to try them on and make sure you like the way they look." She bats her green eyes at me.

"Would you like me to take you shopping when we get home?"

"Please, Daddy."

"I can arrange that." She smiles as I pull her lips to mine.

71

CHAPTER
Eleven

ARIA

The private jet was a new experience. I don't have much to compare it to. I think the last time I was on a plane was when I was seven, maybe eight. It was the last family vacation we took before Luke left and I'm pretty sure I slept the entire flight back then. From the second we boarded until the moment we landed everything was being taken care of for us. Theo seemed used to all of it, even expected it. I could see myself getting used to this type of luxury, but I need to remember Theo will leave. They all do. So I am going to enjoy it while it lasts. Theo is finishing up a phone call when we land. I wait for his instruction. He keeps looking over at me with a mischievous smirk. I am half tempted to start taking clothes off whenever he looks at me. I don't, but next time we fly I'll ask that there not be any additional crew so we can have the plane to ourselves. I'm sure he won't have a problem helping me join the mile-high club, but I'd rather not have an audience.

He ends his call and looks back at me.

"Ready to go Baby girl?"

"If you are." I smile as he reaches out a hand and helps me off the couch. We walk to the front of the plane and down the narrow steps. A black car is waiting for us on the tarmac. Theo's hand never leaves mine as we are quickly ushered into the back seat.

"Things are a little different here than you're used to." Theo tries to explain.

"You mean the private jet and chauffeur?" I tease. "I thought your apartment was nice, apparently you slum it when you're home." He laughs.

"The apartment isn't mine, it belongs to my boss. He let me stay in it while in town." Well, there goes the idea of offering to house-sit. I have a few days away, I need to use this time to figure out how to get out of my mother's house. Going home after disappearing for a few days will be a shit storm, that is if she even realized I was gone.

"Baby, talk to me." Theo's command grabs my attention.

"About what?" I smile, trying to play off whatever he thinks he just saw in my expression.

"Why did the light in your eyes fade when I said the apartment belonged to my boss?" He leans toward me. He knows, I don't know how he knows but he knows. This is going to be really annoying if I can never hide anything from him.

"I was just planning on asking if I could stay in it a little while I figure out my next steps so I wouldn't have to go home. But it's not your place to offer up, so I need a new plan."

His eyes darken, as the car stops. He looks out the window and then back at me, "We will discuss that later, but we're here."

"Here being where?" I ask as I try to look out the window for any sign.

"You said you wanted to go shopping right?" He smiles.

"Now?" I ask in surprise.

"Well you need things, don't you?" The door opens and Theo slides out of the car, before extending his hand to me. I take it as he leads me through an alley and then what seems to be a back entrance to a store. It takes me a minute to realize where we are. I have never seen the inside of this building let alone it devoid of people. Designer clothes are displayed as far as the eye can see. I look up at Theo's face to see him smiling down at me.

"What do I need for the weekend?"

"Don't worry about that, get anything you want."

"Anything?" I cannot contain the excitement.

"Anything." He says again. Standing on my tiptoes I kiss him before letting go of his hand and begin looking through the racks.

Theo sits on the couch in front of the fitting room and pulls out his phone. The attendant takes arms full of clothes to the fitting room for me. Theo doesn't ever even look up from his phone as she places the clothes on the racks. I wonder if he expects it to be her and not me, or if I walked past he would ignore me too. I walk a few racks over until my eyes catch on something that I know will get his attention. I grab several hangers and walk to the fitting room. I walk past Theo, not looking at him for even a second, before I enter the fitting room and close the curtain. Quickly undressing I put on one of the lace teddies I grabbed. This one is a sheer red lace bodysuit. I look at my body in it, I look hot. The red isn't my favorite but it does make a statement. I open the curtain and walk out to the three-way mirror. I stand and look at myself twisting to show different angles, all while watching Theo on the couch behind me. He looks up from his phone for a brief second before his focus returns to his phone. He types out one more thing before putting it down and returning his gaze to me. I can almost feel the burn of his stare as his eyes rake over my body.

"What do you think?" I ask sweetly.

"I think you should come here so I can see better." Walking towards him I stop just before I am within his reach. His eyes focus on me with an intense stare.

"I don't think I like this color on me." I say, turning back to the mirror. I watch as Theo adjusts himself in the reflection. I begin walking away, feeling his eyes on me the entire time. I close the curtain and pull the lace off my body. I pull the white bodysuit off the hanger and slide it onto my body. I already like this one better. I adjust the back so that the thong sits just perfectly between my ass cheeks. I walk back out to the mirror and watch as Theo's gaze hardens. He lifts his hand and curls one finger back. I do as instructed, but again stop just out of reach. This time I turn to the side and bend down to grab the gold heels I had placed next to the couch. I slip them on slowly making sure Theo has a great view of my body. Once they are on I turn to look at myself in the mirror, Theo stands and reaches out for my arm. His smile is telling me exactly what he is thinking, he wants me. I spin back flipping my hair over my shoulder, and putting myself just out of his reach.

"Yes, Daddy?"

"You know exactly what you're doing." I can't help but laugh. "Which means you know what is going to happen." I stand closer to him, to where we are chest to chest.

"Whatever do you mean?" I say as sweetly as possible before turning to head back to the fitting room. The last time I said that Theo fucked me so hard, I saw stars. His hand wraps around my throat pulling me back into him. I smile as his grip tightens.

"Do it again and there will be consequences." He says softly in my ear before letting go of me. He sits back down and I stand between his legs. His fingers gently caress up the sides of my legs just until they hit the lace of the bodysuit. Heels click against the tile floor as the attendant makes her way back into the fitting room.

"You can be excused. I'll call the owner when we are finished." He says loudly, not taking his eyes off me. She quickly turns and walks back the way she came.

I watch as she disappears before returning my attention to Theo.

"There's another outfit I'd like to show you." The frustration in his eyes shows me just how much I am affecting him. He leans back against the couch and I start moving back, very intentional with every one of my steps. Once I'm out of his reach I spin exaggerating my hip movements and swaying them ever so slightly as I walk back to the fitting room. Once the curtain is closed I bring my hand to my neck feeling where his fingerprints would be if he pressed harder. I cannot help but smile as the butterflies fly around in my stomach. Sex with Theo has been amazing but it's more than that. The dynamic between us is nothing like the relationships I've had in the past. The level of trust and compatibility between us is something I never imagined I would have. And we aren't even really a thing. We haven't said we're exclusive but the way he acted the other night at the bar leads me to believe he wants to be, or at least I be exclusively for him. Just the thought of him being able to sleep with other women turns the butterflies to stone. I slide on the black lace, barely hiding anything in this outfit. I'm glad they had several of this set in my size because I want Theo to rip them off of me.

I slide the curtain over in a way that I can elongate my body. As I strut my way across the fitting room, I watch every slight adjustment Theo makes. His eyes roam down my body, stalling at my midriff momentarily before raking his gaze down my legs.

"Beautiful." He mumbles. I spin just out of his reach giving him a view of my half-exposed ass.

"The set really is." I respond.

"You know damn well I wasn't talking about the outfit." His lips lift slightly at the corners. He leans forward and tries to place his hand on my hip. Before he makes contact I swat his hand away. A fire burns in his eyes as he looks up at me. I shake my head "no" as he stands.

Towering over me he looks down at me as prey.

"That is three."

CHAPTER
Twelve

ARIA

"Three what?" I say with a smile widening across my face. I know he won't let this behavior slide but damn is he hot when he looks at me like that. Whatever punishment he deems fit, will be well worth it. He grabs my wrist and pulls me down across his lap as he sits back down.

My knees are pressed against the side of his thigh as I am sprawled across his lap. He now holds both my wrists above my head.

"What do you think the punishment should be for not letting me touch you?" I smile at the thought. He gently slides my hair off my back, so it's all hanging off to one side of my face. He drags his hand slowly down my back until he reaches my ass. He pauses for a moment, before lifting his hand off of me. It returns quickly with a sting as he spanks me. My body jumps with the contact. His grip on my wrist tightens. His hand raises again, bringing it down harder this time. The sharp pain lingers a little longer. My core tightens as he raises his hand again. I brace for the impact. He brings his hand down one last time. I moan as the burn across my ass cheek begins to settle.

"You take your punishment so well." Theo slides his fingers underneath the fabric between my legs, finding me dripping with arousal. He presses his fingers against my entrance, teasing me.

"Daddy." A breathy plea escapes my lips, wanting to feel him inside me. He lets out a soft chuckle, slowly sliding his fingers deeper. I whine as he pulls his finger out and slides them to my clit. My heart begins to race as his fingers circle my clit, building pressure in my core. I wiggle my wrists, but his hand engulfs them and will not let them free.

"So needy." He taunts, moving his fingers slower and slower. "I don't think you deserve to cum, do you?" A slight whimper escapes my mouth when his fingers stop moving completely.

He waits for an answer.

"No, Daddy." I say almost in a whisper.

"On your knees." He commands as he lets my wrists free. I slide off his knees before positioning myself in front of him. He sits taller as he looks down at me. I expect him to undo his belt and pull out his cock, but he just smiles down at me.

"Do you want my dick, Baby girl?" I nod. He leans down, putting his face directly in front of mine, "Only good girls get what they want."

He pulls away and I look up at him through my lashes, "Please Daddy, I'll be good."

He places his hand on the side of my face, gently running his thumb across my bottom lip.

"Oh, I know you will." A devilish smile on his lips. He lowers his hand slightly so it is wrapped around my throat. The slight pressure against my throat has my eyes closing and my mouth falling open with a soft gasp. The ache between my thighs intensifies.

"I want to watch you take my fingers like you take my dick." My eyes shoot open and look at him. "Be a good girl and maybe I'll let you cum."

I swallow hard against his grip which seems to please him. I press my lips together, wetting them slightly as the pressure in my core builds. At this point, it's no longer a want but a need for him to fuck me. And he seems to know it, and he is going to make me earn it, which makes me want it even more.

His free hand slides up the back of my neck grabbing a handful of hair, before roughly pulling my head back, "Open wide sweetheart."

My breath hitches as I do what I'm told. He releases my hair and places his two fingers on my bottom lip. I flick my tongue gently, licking his fingertips. He swallows a groan before pressing his fingers into my mouth. I wrap my lips around him, swirling my tongue around him. If he wants to watch me suck his fingers like I suck his dick I will give him a show. I let out a soft moan as I lift my head, pulling him further into my mouth. His grip on my neck tightens. I slowly draw my head back, sucking his fingers as they slide out of my mouth. He loosens his grip on my throat momentarily, letting me take a deep breath.

"Just like that." He coaches as his hand grips my throat again but in a position of control this time, with his forefinger and thumb lifting my face to look directly at him. My pussy begins to throb, wanting to be touched. I slide one of my hands between my legs to relieve some of the pressure, wanting any kind of release. His eyes drop from my mouth to my hand.

"Did I say you could touch yourself, Baby?" I look up to him, unable to respond. He adjusts his leg so his foot is between my thighs. "Such a needy little slut. Getting face fucked by my fingers has you begging to cum." He lets out a cocky laugh.

I arch my back as I let out a shaky breath, "*Mmmhmm*". I try to nod my head but his grip won't let me move.

He lifts the toe of his shoe pressing it against my clit. My body immediately reacts to the pressure. My hips shift, putting the pressure exactly where I need it. Frantically I roll my hips, my muscles tightening as the pleasure builds. He begins forcing his fingers deeper into my mouth. My eyes begin to water at the intrusion but I can't stop bucking my hips against his shoe. Heat spreads under my skin, I thrust once, twice more. I let out a choked sob, as I am about to cum, when he removes his foot. My body sinks. I whimper around his fingers as he thrusts his fingers harder into my mouth.

"I told you, only good girls get to cum." He whispers above my ear. He holds his fingers at the back of my throat, making me glad I don't have a gag reflex. Tears stream down my face as he pulls his fingers out of my mouth. He drops his hand from my throat and sits back fully on the couch.

I sit back on my heels, hands in my lap, "Please Daddy."

He slowly unbuckles his belt and unbuttons his pants. I watch eagerly as he lowers the zipper. I press my lips together as reaches into his pants and pulls out his fully hard cock. Immediately the heat between my legs returns.

"Have you earned it?" He asks mockingly.

"Please," I beg.

"Please who?" He asks his thumb slowly rubbing the drop of precum around the tip of his dick.

"Please Daddy." I whine.

"Come here, Baby." I jump up to straddle him, but he stops me before I can. "These have to go." He says hooking a finger under the lace waistband. I quickly slide them down my legs, "The top too." I unhook the bra and toss it aside, leaving me in just the gold heels. He grabs my waist and pulls me in, lowering me onto his cock. Straddling him I grab onto his shoulder as he fills me. My head falls back as he lifts his hips and fully disappears into my body.

"You were made for me, Aria." He moans. He slowly drops his hips before thrusting back into me, hard.

"You are mine." He thrusts again, hitting just the right spot. "Do you hear me?"

"Yes, Daddy, I'm yours." I cry out.

He licks his thumb before placing it against my clit, rubbing small circles as he thrusts deeper and deeper inside me. My body tenses and my vision becomes cloudy as my pussy clenches around his cock. He thrusts in one last time harder than before and lets out a strangled grunt. We are both pushed over the edge as he cums inside me.

"Good girl." He says as I ride the waves of aftershock. I fall limp against his chest, breathing heavily. He holds me for a few minutes, running his fingers gently down my back, before saying, "Let's go home Baby Girl."

CHAPTER
Thirteen

THEO

Aria has her arms draped over my shoulders and legs wrapped around my waist as I carry her to the car. I helped her wash her face and put on one of her new outfits before calling Peterson about the tab and letting my driver know we were almost ready to leave. Gerard opens the door allowing me to slide into the back seat without disturbing her. I give Gerard a nod of thanks as he closes the door.

"Baby, I want to talk to you about something." She sleepily pulls her head from my shoulder, to look at me. "I don't want you going back to your mom's."

"Me either, but I don't have a choice, Theo."

"I know this is very new and you aren't sure what you want yet, but I cannot let you go back. I can get you a job at my buddy's company, and let you start earning experience with your degree. We can go apartment shopping and get you your own place. No strings attached."

"What happens when you leave?" My heart breaks as she raises this concern. My fingers immediately brush the strands of blonde hair from her face, before placing my hand against her face. She leans into the touch, a swell of pride fills my chest.

"I'm not going anywhere Baby girl." I assure her. "I want you near me, I want you safe and happy. But I also want you to get everything you want in life, even if it's not me." Her eyes focus on me, unsure of what to say.

"I can send someone to pack your things at your mom's and have it shipped wherever you choose. Please let me provide this for you."

"Okay." she whispers, "On one condition." She grabs my hand and rests in her lap.

"Anything."

"I want to move in with you." She says so softly.

I take my hand from her and pull her lips to mine. I kiss her like I've never kissed anyone before. This kiss means so much more than just physical affection. She fully trusts me. She wants me. She wants to be with me.

The car comes to a stop.

"Then let's go show you your new home." I say against her lips. She smiles as the door opens. Gerard extends a hand helping her to her feet as I exit the back seat. She has her head craned to the sky, looking at my- our building.

"Let me guess. The penthouse?"

"That would be correct. Let's introduce you to Enzo at the front desk. I want to inform him that you will be moving in, and should be treated accordingly." I guide her toward the glass doors being held open by security.

She looks a little apprehensive but excited.

We walk in and head toward the marble desk in the center of the lobby.

"Mr. Reeves, Welcome home." Enzo stands behind the desk as I approach.

"I hope everything was uneventful while I was gone." He smiles.

"No issues sir."

"Good to hear. Enzo, this is Aria. She will be staying with me for the foreseeable future. She is to have full access, and be treated like you treat me." He nods, as Aria stands to the side of me.

"Aria, Enzo is head of security. He also oversees the concierge team. If you need anything, let him know and it will be handled." She nods nervously.

"It's nice to meet you." Her voice shakes a little but I doubt Enzo heard as the phone rang. He politely nods before answering the call. We start to head toward the private elevator at the back of the lobby when his voice catches my attention.

"Mr. Reeves. You have company waiting for you. They went up roughly thirty minutes ago." I nod and thank him while leading Aria into the elevator. She looks up at me with a questioning look. I press my wallet to the scanner before pressing the 'Penthouse' button.

"It's either my business partner or boss. I'm sure it's something I can handle quickly. When we get inside I want you to be polite. Say hello, but I want you to go to my- our room and stay there until I come to get you." I instruct. This shouldn't be anything too serious but I do not want her caught up in the middle of whatever it is. As much as I want her to be a permanent fixture in my life, she cannot know about my work. It will put her in too much danger, especially if she decides to leave. She nods her head.

The elevator doors open into my living room and as I expected Maddox and Russel are sitting on my couch, whiskey glasses in hand.

"Gentleman." I greet them as we walk into the window-lined room. Both of them look at me and immediately notice Aria standing just behind me.

"This is Aria. Aria meet Garret Maddox and Tatum Russel. They run the association I am a part of." Not a lie, but definitely not the full truth. If anything they run two-thirds of The Court and Garret is engaged to the other third.

"Pleasure to meet you." She extends her hand to both the men, giving a very confident handshake. "I don't mean to be rude, but it was a long trip so I am going to excuse myself to get freshened up a bit." She comes back to me and presses a gentle kiss on my cheek before I lead in the direction of the bedroom.

Both men watch as she walks away. Once the door shuts they look back at me expecting an explanation.

"She is new." Garret says, his tone light, giving me a clue that the reason they are here isn't as serious as I was expecting. I relax a bit by taking off my jacket and laying it over the back of the couch.

"How did going to Texas to deal with shitty lawyers turn into you bringing home a girl that is way out of your league?" Tatum chuckles.

"Long story, which I don't think we have time for since you needed to drop by in the middle of the night." Garret nods before placing his glass down on the table. Their demeanor changed almost instantly.

"We have a problem."

The End

If you loved Call Him Daddy and need to know what happens next, get ready for the spicy sequel:

Keep My Secrets

Theo Reeves never worried about how he would explain his profession to a partner; he never planned on letting anyone get that close. Now that he not only has feelings for the blonde half his age but also moved her across state lines to be with him, it's only a matter of time before the truth has to come out.

Aria Mason never expected to have a whirlwind romance with anyone, let alone her mother's ex-fiancée. After a chance encounter, a bar bathroom, and an undeniable connection, she did exactly that, finding herself in the penthouse of the most exclusive building in the city. He says he wants to provide for her, but with all the quiet phone calls and extended work trips it seems they may end just as fast as the started unless he can trust her to Keep His Secrets.

———

Pre Order Now

Acknowledgments

I tried to keep this novella short and spicy, so I will try to keep these acknowledgments short and sweet.

Bria, you truly are an irreplaceable part of my team. This book would not have been made if I hadn't had you in my corner. Thank you. Thank you for your support, your dedication, and all your hard work. You are amazing and I am so lucky to have you not only on my team but in my life.

Alina, I am so proud of all the things you are accomplishing. You inspire me more than you know. Thank you for your beautiful outlook on life, your unwavering support, and the way you love me and my little family. Our calls are always a highlight of my week.

Emily, Thank you for jumping in and wanting to be a part of this journey with me. Thank you for helping make this book possible.

Renee, Not only have you taught me so much about the author journey but you also raised my real-life book boyfriend. I will never be able to thank you enough for raising the man of my dreams.

Crystal and Micheal, Your support from the beginning has meant so much to me. Thank you for being on this journey with me and taking a chance on this baby author. Your support has been the reason my books have been made.

Thank you to all my new patrons who have joined this journey recently! The best is yet to come!

To my Street Team, You guys are the absolute best hype

team a girl could ever ask for. Thank you for encouraging me, motivating me, and laughing with me. Thank you for being excited about all the little announcements and for always being up for hearing out my crazy ideas. I love all of you.

To My ARC readers, Thank you for caring about my book. Thank you for taking time out of your busy schedules to read and review my book. Your feedback inspires me to keep writing.

To all my readers, Thank you. There aren't enough words to express how grateful I am for you. There will never be enough time to finish our TBRs, yet you chose to read my story. Thank you for caring about what I have to say and the characters I have created.

Until next time, drink your water, be gentle with yourself, and fall in love with every new story.

Veni.Vidi.Amavi.

About the Author

Katie Perez lives with her husband and 2 young children.

She is known for her dark and angsty romances, filled with strong women, powerful men, and the spice that carries them into their happily ever after.

When she is not daydreaming of all the stories to add to the Acadia Universe, she is either gardening or hyper-focusing on learning a new skill.

Also By Katie A Perez

A Fake Dating Insta-Love Holiday Romance

Meet Me On The Mountainside

www.ingramcontent.com/pod-product-compliance
Lightning Source LLC
Chambersburg PA
CBHW072011170626
46813CB00005B/2114